SCARY RAPS

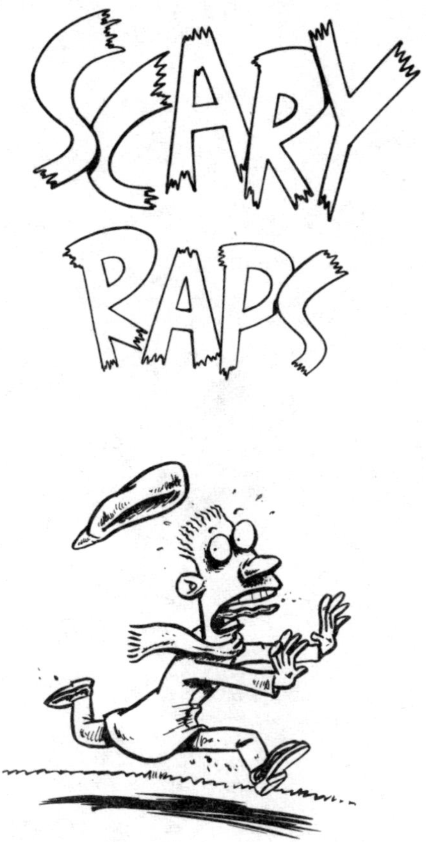

To Andrew & Sheena Matthews
from TM and family,
with love

ORCHARD BOOKS
96 Leonard Street, London EC2A 4XD
Orchard Books Australia
14 Mars Road, Lane Cove, NSW 2066
First published in Great Britain in 1999
First Paperback publication 2000
Text © Tony Mitton 1999
Illustrations © Martin Chatterton 1999
The rights of Tony Mitton to be identified as the author
and Martin Chatterton as the illustrator of this work
have been asserted by them in accordance with the
Copyright, Designs and Patents Act, 1988.
A CIP catalogue record for this book is available
from the British Library.
1 84121 151 6 (hardback)
1 84121 153 2 (paperback)

Tony Mitton

SCARY RAPS

illustrated by Martin Chatterton

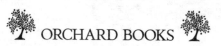 ORCHARD BOOKS

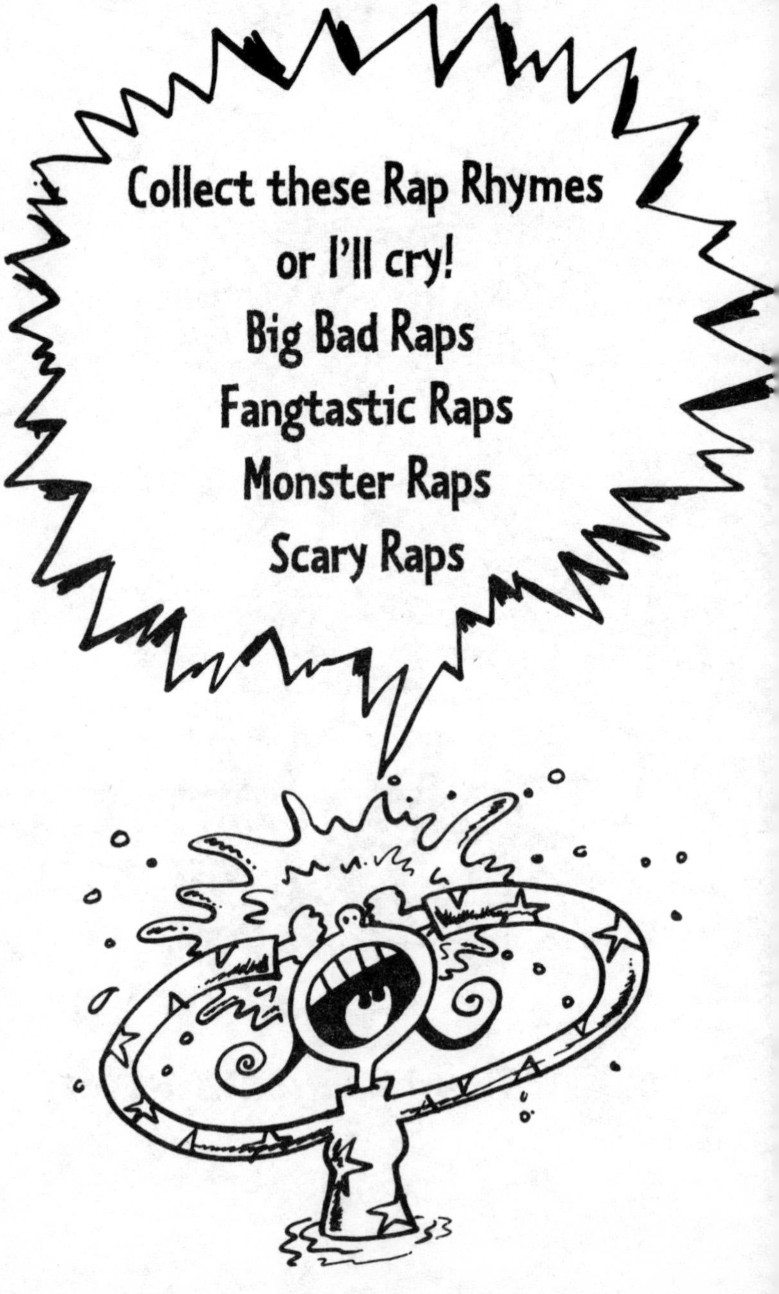
Collect these Rap Rhymes
or I'll cry!
Big Bad Raps
Fangtastic Raps
Monster Raps
Scary Raps

CONTENTS

In the gas-lit lanes
of London Town,
when the streets were cobbled
and the fog was brown,

there lived a guy
called Dr Jeck.
And was he clever?
Yes, by heck!

When it came to chemistry
he was fab.
He could do all kinds
of things in his lab.

He could make a snake
look like a rat.
He could turn a dog
into a cat.

He could get a girl
to grow a beard.
He could make a guy
look really weird.
And he might've won
the Nobel Prize
if he hadn't had
such ugly eyes.

"The Nobel Prize?
What's that?" you say.
It's the prize for which
all boffins pray.
Just win that prize,
you've made your name.
Yes, that's the way
to world-wide fame.

"If it wasn't for
my ugly looks,"
said Jeck, "I'd be
in all the books.
My big, round eyes
look kind of…mad.
And maybe even
rather bad."

9

So he took some bottles
off his shelf,
saying, "Now it's time
to change MYSELF!

I'll fix it so
I have The Look."
Then he put his potions
on to cook.
"We'll start with good old
CO_2.
And how about Handsome
Crystals, too?

"Some H2O will
help it hubble.
And aftershave
should cause no trouble.

A little stir
with eyelash stick –
I'll soon look like
a fashion pic.
And all those other
boffin guys
will let me have
that Nobel Prize."

And he mumbled and muttered
through the night
as he made his brew
exactly right.

So soon it stood there,
strange and fizzy.
"Yo!" said Jeck.
"Now let's get busy."

He put the potion
to his lips.
He shut his eyes
and tried two sips.
"Hmmm…" he said,
"well, here goes. Ulp!"
With that he took
a great big gulp.

His body did
a funny jig.
And then he took
a final swig.

He swayed and tumbled.
Crumple, crash!
His legs and arms
began to thrash.

And then he had
a sneezing fit.
"OK," he sniffed,
"this must be it."

14

He gave the mirror
a wary eye.
"Strange…" he murmured.
"Where am I…?

But, hey!" he gasped,
"Can this be me?
This fashion icon
that I see?
Look! No more wrinkles,
no more bags.
This face will fit
the fashion mags.

The potion's even
changed my suit.
Well, that should save me
lots of loot.

Sad Jeck is dead!"
he proudly cried.
"From now I'm handsome
Mr Hide."

And so he posed there,
looking good,
imagining
the things he could,
like how he'd wow
those boffin guys
and waltz off with
the Nobel Prize,

and how the crowds
would clap and cheer
and vote him Cool Prof
Of The Year.

But just a minute…
Hey! What's this?
His ears began
to steam and hiss.

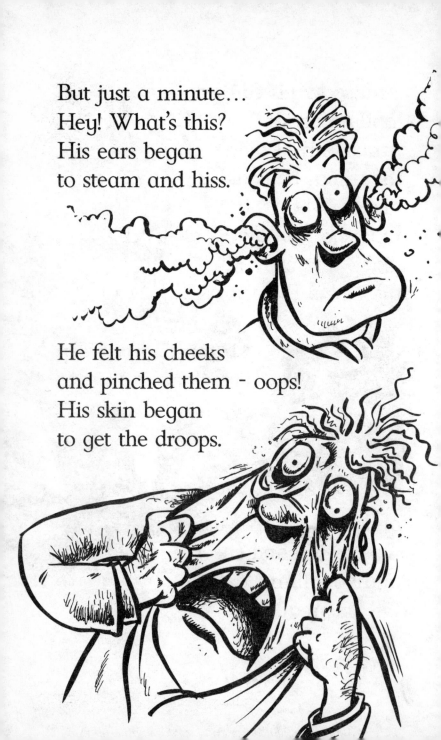

He felt his cheeks
and pinched them - oops!
His skin began
to get the droops.

And now his fine
and fancy kit
looked like it didn't
really fit.

"Oh no!" he gulped,
beginning to weep.
"I'm worse than ever:
a real creep!

And what's this happening
in my brain?
That drink is turning
me insane."

He shook his head
and gave a roar.
Then creepy Hide
crashed through the door.

The bubbly brew
had turned his mind
and made him start
to feel unkind.
He'd thought that it
would make him hip.
Instead the stuff
had made him flip.

And as we cut
to change the scene,
you'll find him acting
really mean.
He frightened folk
along the streets.
He ran in shops
and stole the sweets.

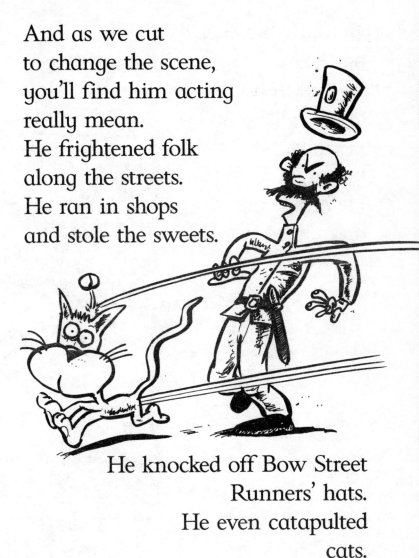

He knocked off Bow Street
Runners' hats.
He even catapulted
cats.

He did what nice guys
never do.
He hid in doorways
then cried, "Boo!"
He gave the local
kids a scare.
He broke their toys
and pulled their hair.

His horrid shape
grew slowly worse.
I think I even
heard him curse.

He rolled in rubbish
till he stank.
And then he went
and robbed a bank.

Well, that was it.
The Bow Street Boys
came running up
to stop the noise.

Said horrid Hide,
"It's time to dash."
He crammed his clothes
with loads of cash.

Then off he ran.
The Boys gave chase.
But, as they did,
Hide's horrid face
began to droop
yet even more.
"Oh, dang!" he cursed.
"Now that's a bore."

"Stop!" he called.
"I'm out of breath.
I need a rest.
I feel like death."
The Boys stood still
without a sound.
For Hide was melting
to the ground.

25

They tried to put
the handcuffs on.
But nope. No use.
His hands were gone.

His clothes became
a messy muddle.
And Hide himself
was soon a puddle.

And as he gurgled
clean away,
a Bow Street Boy
was heard to say,
"There's no one left here
to arrest.
The case is closed.
We did our best."

So that's the end.
And here's the heap
of clothes that once
were Hide the Creep.

Over the dark
and dreary moors
there hangs a hush,
there comes a pause…

And then there echoes
round and round
the baying of
a ghostly hound.

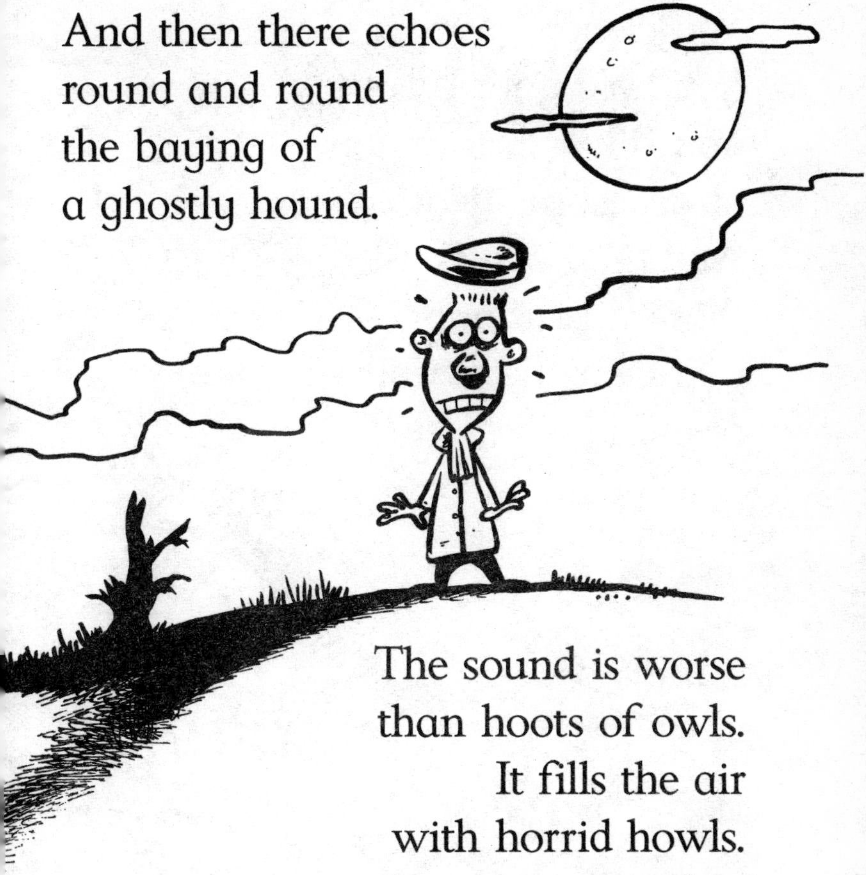

The sound is worse
than hoots of owls.
It fills the air
with horrid howls.
It makes your skin
begin to thrill,
and then your blood
turns cold and chill.

You clench your fists.
You hold your breath.
You fill with thoughts
of gruesome death.
And then across
those misty moors
you hear the pound
of giant paws.

You hear a snarl.
You see it bound.
It is a great
ferocious hound.
It hurtles swiftly
into view,
and then you see
it's after you!

The sight of it
can strike you dead.
Or leave you barmy
in the head.
It is the grossest
beast of all.
It is The Hound
of Basket Hall!

Doc Watson put
his News away
and thoughtfully
began to say,

"A hound that seems more ghost than dog. A hound that hunts poor souls through fog. A hound that spooks the moors with moans. This is a case for Sherlock Bones."

His friend put down
his violin
and gave a cool
and clever grin.

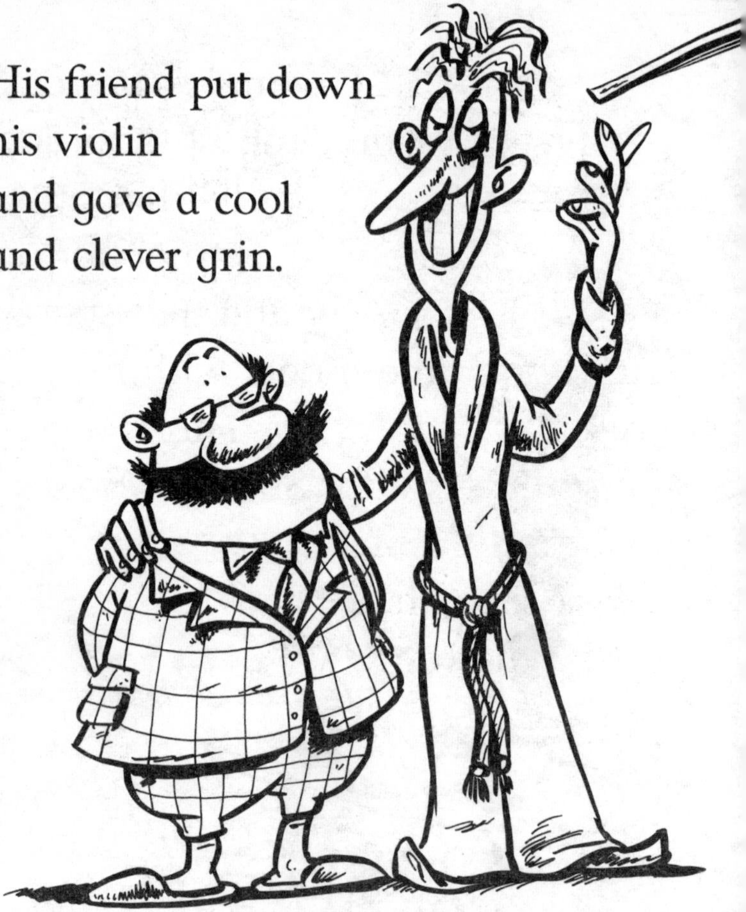

"A ghostly hound?
We'll soon fix that.
Let's boogie, Watson.
Grab your hat."

And soon they both
sat on the train
which puffed along
to Basket Plain,
where later they
sat by the fire
of old Lord Basket,
local squire.

His butler served
a swell cream tea
and helped to tell
the mystery.

Then just as dusk
began to fall
they heard the hound
begin to call.

Said Watson, "Bones,
let's stay indoors.
I hear the pound
of giant paws."
But Bones snapped back,
"No time for fear.
I think I have
a Big Idea.

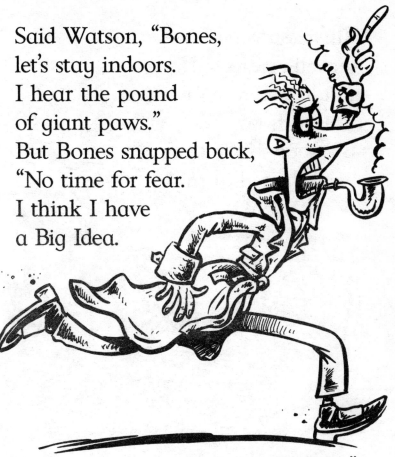

So bring the bag,"
Doc heard him shout.
"Let's hit the moors
and check this out."

The moors were weird
and full of fog.
The moors were marshy,
wet with bog.
But though the trails
were draped in mist
Bones wore a compass
on his wrist.

And carefully
they tracked the sound
that seemed to tremble
through the ground.

Quite soon they heard
a tap, tap, tap.
Bones shone a torch
upon his map.
"Aha!" he smiled.
"Just as I thought.
This hound of ours
will soon be caught."

"Watch out!" cried Doc
as through the fog
came flying an
enormous dog.

But from his bag
Bones snatched a ball,
and threw it with
a real cool call.

"Loose ball," he yelled,
and ball and dog
went bouncing off
through mist and fog.

"That's strange," said Doc.
"The hound is gone.
And yet his paws
pound on and on..."

"Aha!" rapped Bones
His eyes grew bright.
He turned his torch
and shone its light.
To Doctor Watson's
great surprise
a mine stood there
before their eyes.

To drain the mine
there beat a pump.
It made a steady
THUMP - KERFLUMP!
They'd thought the THUMP -
KERFLUMPING sound
was giant paws
that beat the ground,

but it was just
a loud machine
that kept the mine
both dry and clean.

Beside the mine
a man, quite old,
was carrying
a crate of gold.
"Just keep away!"
they heard him whine.
"It is not yours.
It's mine, all mine."

"The butler guy
who served us tea!"
cried Bones. "This solves
our mystery.

He put that horrid
tale about
to stop us all
from finding out
that on his master's
moors he'd found
a mine of gold
beneath the ground.

And here's his hound,
not fierce at all.
Just look, he's bringing
back our ball."

When they got back
Lord Basket said,
"Well, I'll be danged!"
and scratched his head.
"This gold I've got's
amazing stuff.
I can't have paid
my man enough.

The poor old guy
is eighty-three.
Besides, he makes
fantastic tea.

We'll go on living
on the moors.
What's mine is his
and also yours.
So have as much
as you can hold.
Who cares? It's only
lumps of gold.

But hey! You're here
at Basket Hall.
C'mon. Let's play
some basketball!"